LARA CROFT TOMB RAIDER
TECH MANUAL

BRYCE TURING WITH MICHAEL JAN FRIEDMAN

POCKET BOOKS

NEW YORK LONDON TORONTO SYDNEY SINGAPORE

An *Original* Publication of POCKET BOOKS

Pocket Books, a division of Simon & Schuster, Inc.
1230 Avenue of the Americas, New York, NY 10020

    OCT 1 4 2004

This book is published by Pocket Books, a division of Simon & Schuster, Inc., under exclusive license from Paramount Pictures.

ISBN: 0-7434-2354-2

First Pocket Books trade paperback printing June 2001

10 9 8 7 6 5 4 3 2 1

POCKET and colophon are registered trademarks of Simon & Schuster, Inc.

Design: Joseph Omar Ibrahim / Red Herring Design

Printed in the U.S.A.

Acknowledgments

I 'd like to thank the film makers behind *Lara Croft: Tomb Raider.*

I would like to express my gratitude to Margaret Clark, the erstwhile editor of this volume, for her creativity, her dedication, and her fortitude. Without Margaret's contribution, this would have been a dull parade of facts and figures, scarcely worth the reader's notice. I would also like to recognize the efforts of Scott Shannon, our director, for his unwavering support of this and so many other projects. I should also mention all other folks at Pocket Books who were able to make this possible; Judith Curr, Kara Welsh, Donna O'Neill, Penny Haynes, Twisne Fan, and Linda Dingler.

A special thanks goes to Joseph Omar Ibrahim at Red Herring Design for doing such a masterful job of putting all the pieces together and making this book.

Finally, I would like to thank Bryce Turing, my "collaborator," whose ingenuity we celebrate on every page.

—Michael Jan Friedman

INTRODUCTION

I first met Lara Croft, aka Lady Croft, aka the Tomb Raider, on a sullen morning in April. Or maybe it was May, I forget. At any rate, it was raining, I'm pretty sure of that, at least. One of those soft rains that just tickled the roof, barely making it out of the mist category.

When Lara realized what I could do with a circuit board and a little capital, she invited me to work for her. And that's what I've been doing ever since—slaving away in a trailer outside her mansion, coming up with all manner of gadgetry for Lady Croft's forays into the unknown.

In return, she keeps me knee deep in pizza and coffee, and writes a check every time I crave a new toy. Not a bad deal, if I say so myself. A lot better than what Aunt Tilly predicted for me when I turned my back on University.

"Brycie," she said, "you'll never amount to anything if you don't get a good education. And a proper suit, while you're at it. And comb your hair, you look like a houligan."

Lovely woman, my aunt.

Of course, it's not *all* glamor. Lady Croft may have a servant—a fellow named Hillary who wears a suit that would impress Aunt Tilly no end—but there's no room for servants in my trailer. There's only enough room for me and my circuit boards and the occasional gastroenterologist...

Though now that I think about it, that's perhaps one story better left untold.

—BRYCE TURING

AUDIO TRANSCRIPT

TRANSMIT RECEIVE RECORD

LARA: It's hard to read you, Bryce. You need to do something about this damned headset.

BRYCE: And other items as well, I should think. We've got to get you into the twenty-first century.

LARA: I'm a little busy now for details. Speak to you later.

BRYCE: Ta.

COME UP WITH A FEW NIFTY
ODDS & ENDS.
OTHERWISE, SHE'LL WONDER
WHAT I'VE BEEN UP TO.

EMAIL   FILE

CHECK MAIL   COMPOSE   SEND   ATTACH FILE

BRYCE: WELCOME HOME, LADY CROF
              STEP INTO MY LABORATORY
              FIGURATIVELY SPEAKING, OF

[CLICK ON IMAGE FOR CLOSE-UP]

INSTANT MESSAGE

FILE EDIT INSERT PEOPLE

LARA: ANOTHER HALF DOZEN MONITORS, BRYCE?
          WHAT DO THEY DO?

geostationary limit

LUNAR_X

ADXSAE9

ex995

tr13823 016.651 160.906
geostat 5000wm
speed 11.2k/s
16/01/1414 wm

aex1762

gfc14

16456

P29104

active orbits

9931/736-21/23	2231/663-19	
6328/032-86/21	9931/736-21	
6432/542-55/74	6328/032-86	
7676/452-60/43	6432/542-65	
6437/180-38/12	7676/452-60	
5647/929-38/01	6437/180-38	
0980/246-42/33	5647/929-38	
9746/345-54/27	0980/246-42	
0049/274-61/61	9746/345-54	
0383/626-42/39	0049/274-61	

0	.127	200	14.142
1	.270	200	14.142
2	.413	200	14.142
3	.556	200	14.142
4	.699	200	14.142
5	.8		
6	.9		
7	1.12		
8	1.27		
9	1.41		
10	1.55		

INSTANT MESSAGE

FILE EDIT INSERT PEOPLE

BRYCE: THEY TRACK DATA FROM ALL OVER THE WORLD—
WEATHER, TROOP MOVEMENTS, THE WHEREABOUTS
OF YOUNG WOMEN WHO FORGET TO COME IN OUT OF
THE RAIN SOMETIMES.

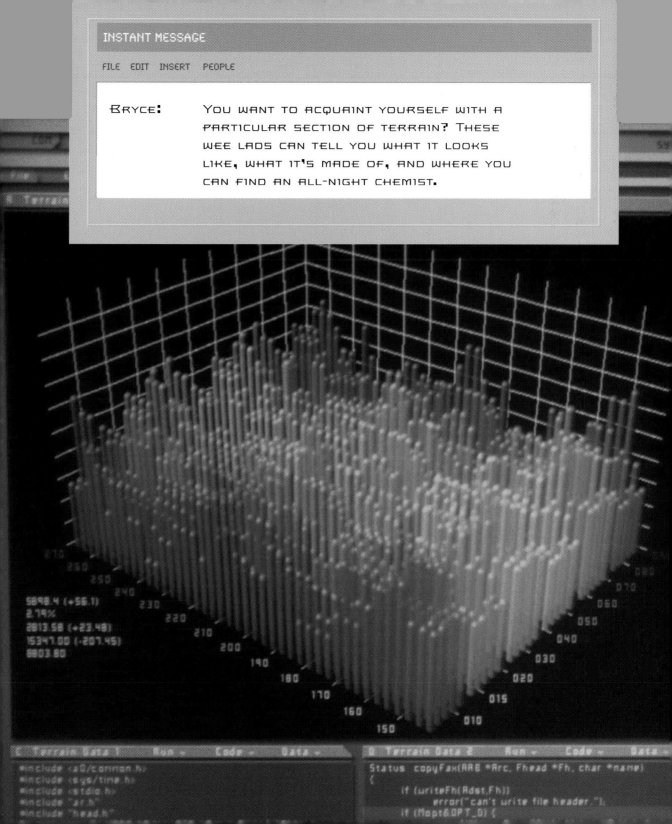

And these bad boys can access the same data anywhere in the world.

Perfect for tomb raiding, don't you think?

INSTANT MESSAGE

FILE   EDIT   INSERT   PEOPLE

BRYCE: You want to visit Cambodia? Here it is, have a go at it—though for the life of me, I can't imagine why you'd want to. They've got worse weather than we do, and that's saying something.

FILE   EDIT   INSERT   PEOPLE

BRYCE: THESE BLOKES ALSO INTERFACE WITH YOUR NEW
           SECURITY SYSTEM.

LARA: I HAVE A NEW SECURITY SYSTEM?

BRYCE: YOU DO INDEED. AND DON'T THANK ME—THAT
           LOOK OF ADMIRATION ON YOUR FACE IS
           THANKS ENOUGH.

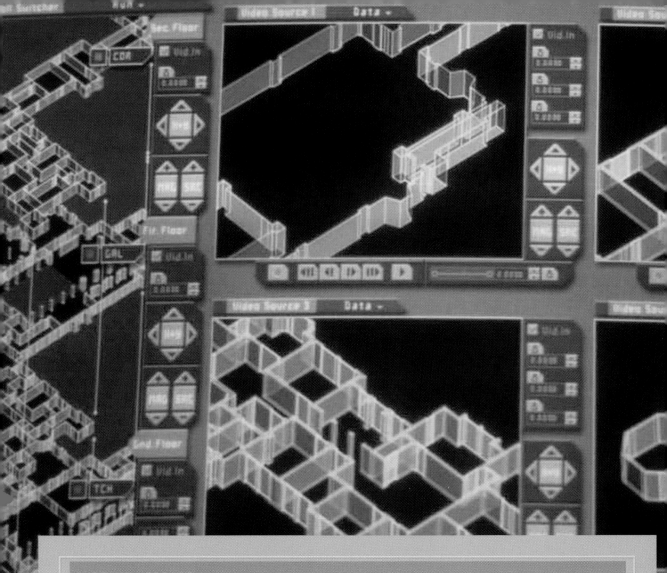

INSTANT MESSAGE

FILE   EDIT   INSERT   PEOPLE

BRYCE: AS YOU CAN SEE, EVERY SQUARE CENTIMETER
            OF THE PLACE IS UNDER ELECTRONIC SURVEILLANCE.

LARA: INCLUDING MY DRESSING ROOM?

BRYCE: WELL ALMOST EVERY SQUARE CENTIMETER.

FILE   EDIT   INSERT   PEOPLE

LARA: AND WHAT HAPPENS TO ALL THIS
          DATA PROCESSING POWER IF WE
          LOSE THE ELECTRIC...HMM?

LIVE FEED

00:00:00

POWER   RECORD PLAY REWIND FORWARD

INSTANT MESSAGE

FILE EDIT INSERT PEOPLE

BRYCE: HOW ABOUT "ROACH CAM"?

LARA: HOW ABOUT NO?

AUDIO TRANSCRIPT

TRANSMIT   RECEIVE   RECORD

BRYCE: AND LEST WE FORGET THAT
          THE BEST DEFENSE IS
          A SMASHING OFFENSE . . .

LARA: YOU'VE MODIFIED MY .45S.

BRYCE: YES I HAVE. I'VE ADDED A CLIP,
          A SIGHT FOR GREATER . . .

LARA: IT'S NOT MY STYLE.

LIVE FEED

AUDIO TRANSCRIPT

TRANSMIT   RECEIVE   RECORD

BRYCE:	OF COURSE IT'S NOT. BUT THIS VARIATION IS MOST CERTAINLY . . .
LARA:	NO AGAIN.

00:00:00

POWER

RECORD PLAY REWIND FORWARD

AUDIO TRANSCRIPT

TRANSMIT   RECEIVE   RECORD

BRYCE: WHAT ABOUT

LARA: DON'T EVEN THINK ABOUT IT,
            BRYCE. I LIKE MY .45S JUST
            THE WAY THEY ARE.

BUT IF YOU LIKE
YOU CAN WHIP UP
SOMETHING
FOR HILLARY.

LIVE FEED

00:00:00

POWER   RECORD PLAY REWIND FORWARD

NOTE TO SELF:
SCRATCH THE .45 MODIFICATIONS,
WORK ON TELESCOPE INSTEAD

LIVE FEED

00:00:00

POWER   RECORD PLAY REWIND FORWARD

EMAIL

CHECK MAIL COMPOSE SEND ATTACH FILE

LARA: I'D LIKE TO GET INTO THE LIBRARY
           AGAIN SOMEDAY. WHAT IN
           BLAZES ARE YOU UP TO?

           YOUR IMPATIENT EMPLOYER, LARA
           P.S. YOUR COLA ARRIVED.

TOO INDUSTRIAL-LOOKING?
NEED ADDITIONAL FOCAL LENGTH?
WILL THE BLASTED THING FIT OR
AM I GOING TO HAVE TO REDESIGN
THE WHOLE BLOODY MANSION?

LIVE FEED

00:00:00

POWER   RECORD PLAY REWIND FORWARD

INSTANT MESSAGE

FILE   EDIT   INSERT   PEOPLE

LARA: CAN I TAKE A LOOK NOW?

BRYCE: BY ALL MEANS. JUST DON'T TELL THE
            TWITS AT NASA—THEY MIGHT GET
            JEALOUS.

INSTANT MESSAGE

FILE   EDIT   INSERT   PEOPLE

LARA: IT'S NOT HUBBLE,
             BUT IT'S CLOSE.

LIVE FEED

00:00:00

POWER   RECORD PLAY REWIND FORWARD

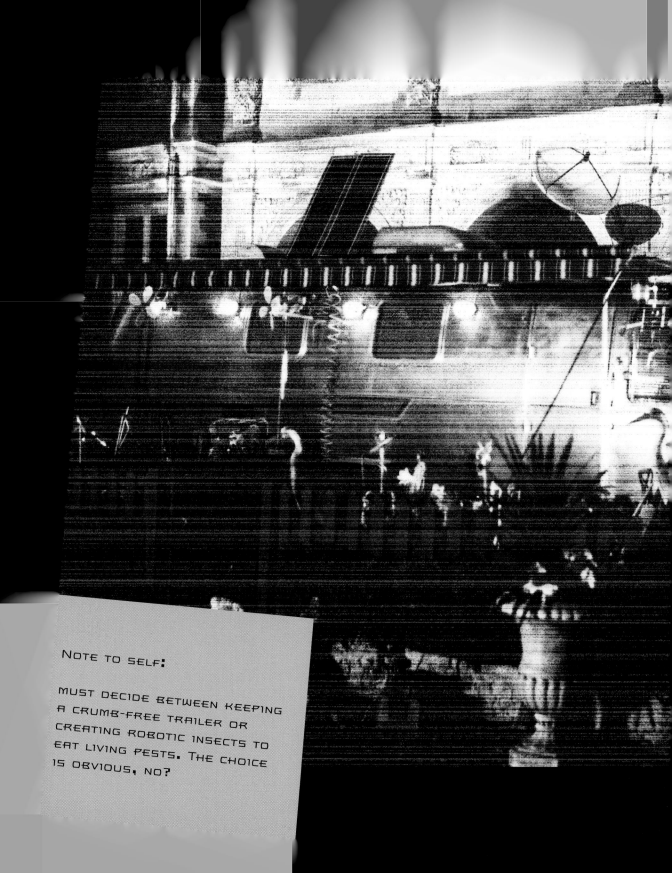

NOTE TO SELF:

MUST DECIDE BETWEEN KEEPING
A CRUMB-FREE TRAILER OR
CREATING ROBOTIC INSECTS TO
EAT LIVING PESTS. THE CHOICE
IS OBVIOUS, NO?

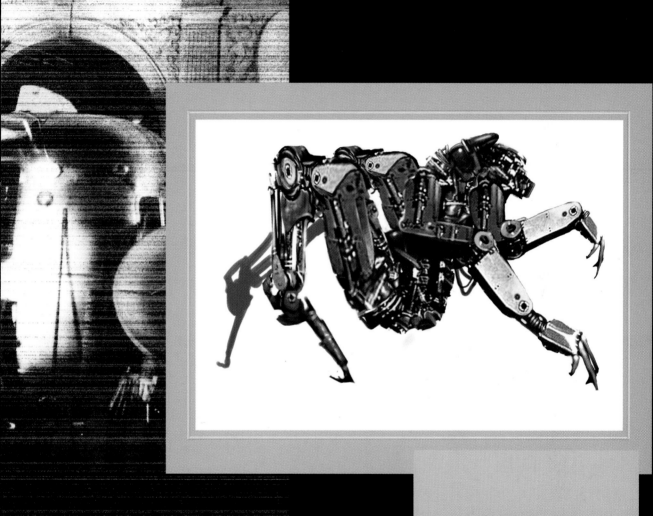

REMINDS ME OF UNCLE
MORT EXCEPT FOR ALL
THE LEGS, OF COURSE.
NOW, AS FOR THE
CYBERNETICS...

THERE WE GO. ECONOMICAL
AND EFFICIENT—EVERY TRAILER
HOME SHOULD HAVE THEM.

LIVE FEED

00:00:00

POWER   RECORD PLAY REWIND FORWARD

INSTANT MESSAGE

FILE   EDIT   INSERT   PEOPLE

LARA: FOUND SOMETHING MECHANICAL IN THE LIBRARY, SMASHED IT TO BITS. IS IT YOURS?

BRYCE: YES HE'S MINE—AND DID YOU HAVE TO KILL HIM? COULDN'T YOU HAVE JUST INCAPACITATED HIM A LITTLE?

LARA: IT'S DEAD. GET OVER IT. AND DON'T LET ME CATCH ANY MORE OF THEM RUNNING AROUND, OR I'M LIABLE TO FORGET HOW HELPFUL YOU ARE.

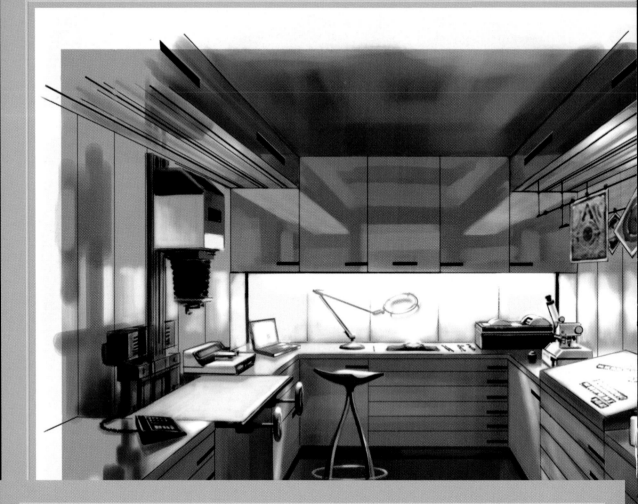

FILE   EDIT   INSERT   PEOPLE

BRYCE: AND HERE I WENT TO THE TROUBLE OF REDESIGNING YOUR
           PHOTO LAB. DON'T YOU FEEL JUST THE LEAST BIT GUILTY NOW?

LARA: TRUTHFULLY?

BRYCE: NEVER MIND.

LIVE FEED

00:00:00

POWER RECORD PLAY REWIND FORWARD

Lara's Photolab

Lara's Photolab (red light)

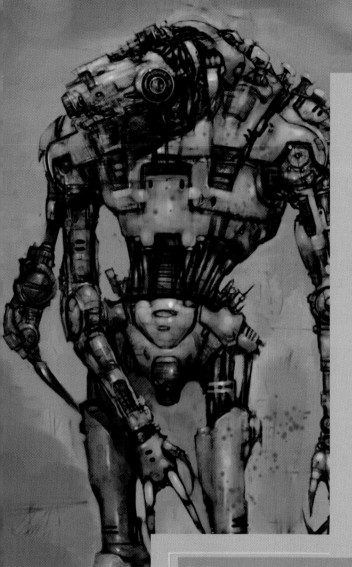

CHECK MAIL   COMPOSE   SEND   ATTACH FILE

BRYCE: THIS ONE'S GOING TO MAKE YOU
            FORGET THE INSECTS.

LARA: IT LOOKS LIKE A ROBOT.

BRYCE: AREN'T YOU THE CLEVER ONE.
            I CALL HIM THE TR1000 OR SIMON
            FOR SHORT.

EMAIL

CHECK MAIL   COMPOSE   SEND   ATTACH FILE

BRYCE: LIKE HIM? HE WIPES
              THE FLOOR WITH
              UNSUSPECTING
              PHOTOJOURNALISTS.

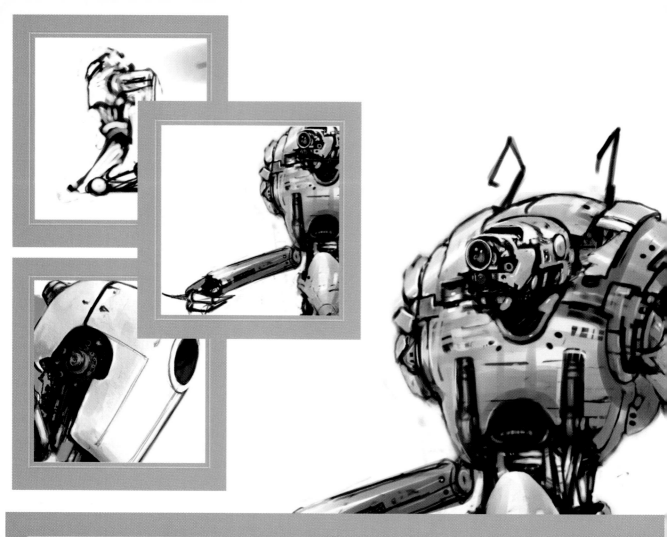

BRYCE: COME NOW, LARA. YOU'VE BEEN COMPLAINING ABOUT A LACK OF GOOD SPARRING PARTNERS. NOW YOU'LL NEVER HAVE TO COMPLAIN AGAIN.

LARA: ACTUALLY, I FEEL A COMPLAINT COMING ON ALREADY.

BRYCE: WHAT? WHAT ARE YOU TALKING ABOUT? IT'S GENIUS. IT'S <u>PERFECT.</u>

INSTANT MESSAGE

FILE   EDIT   INSERT   PEOPLE

LARA: IT'S TOP-HEAVY. A COUPLE OF GOOD IMPACTS
        TO ITS LEGS AND IT WILL FALL LIKE A SACK OF
        POTATOES. ALSO, LOSE THE CLAWS. IF IT CAN'T
        HIT, CUT, OR FIRE, I DON'T WANT TO KNOW ABOUT IT.

        IF I WERE YOU, ACTUALLY, I'D START FROM SCRATCH.

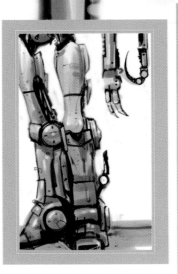

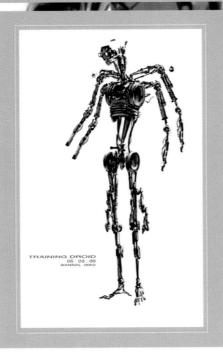

TRAINING DROID
05 . 03 . 00
BANSAL 0002

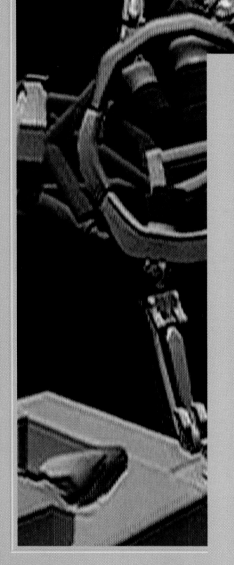

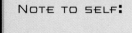

NOTE TO SELF:

START ROBOT DESIGNS
FROM SCRATCH.

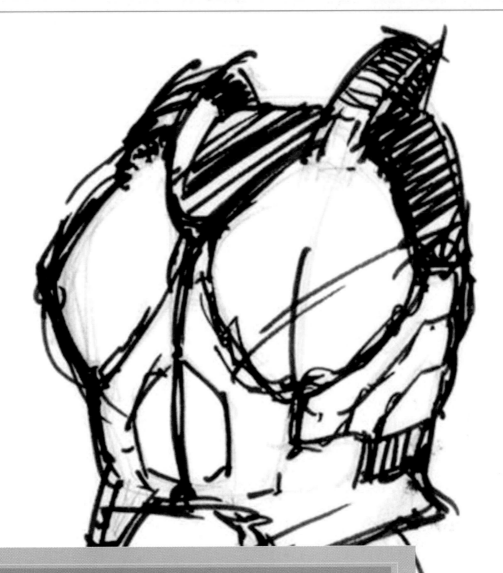

FILE EDIT INSERT PEOPLE

LARA: WHAT'S THIS, NOW?

BRYCE: A KEVLAR VEST. ALL THE TOP
             ADVENTURERS ARE WEARING
             ONE THIS SEASON.

LARA: KEVLAR ISN'T MY STYLE.

BRYCE: ARE BULLET HOLES YOUR STYLE?

FILE   EDIT   INSERT   PEOPLE

LARA: SORRY. NO VEST.

BRYCE: GIVE ME ONE GOOD REASON YOU WOULDN'T
             WANT TO WEAR SOMETHING LIGHTWEIGHT
             AND BULLETPROOF, GIVEN YOUR PROPENSITY FOR
             MEETING UP WITH BLACKGUARDS EVERYWHERE YOU GO.

LIVE FEED

00:00:00

POWER   RECORD PLAY REWIND FORWARD

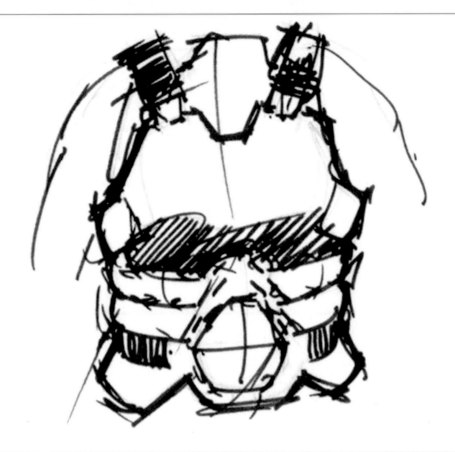

FILE   EDIT   INSERT   PEOPLE

LARA: THE PROBLEM WITH A BULLETPROOF VEST IS YOU COME
          TO RELY ON IT. I'D MUCH RATHER RELY ON <u>MYSELF</u>.

BRYCE: YOU KNOW, WHEN YOU PUT IT THAT WAY, IT ALMOST
          MAKES SENSE.

LARA: NONETHELESS, I THINK I'D LIKE ONE.

BRYCE: YOU WOULD?

LARA: YES—FOR HILLARY.

FILE   EDIT   INSERT   PEOPLE

BRYCE: YOU CARE MORE ABOUT HILLARY THAN YOU DO ME?

LARA: FINE, BRYCIE—YOU CAN HAVE A KEVLAR VEST TOO.

BRYCE: I DON'T WANT ONE. I JUST WANTED TO SEE IF YOU'D
           GET ME ONE.

LARA: BUGGER OFF, YOU.

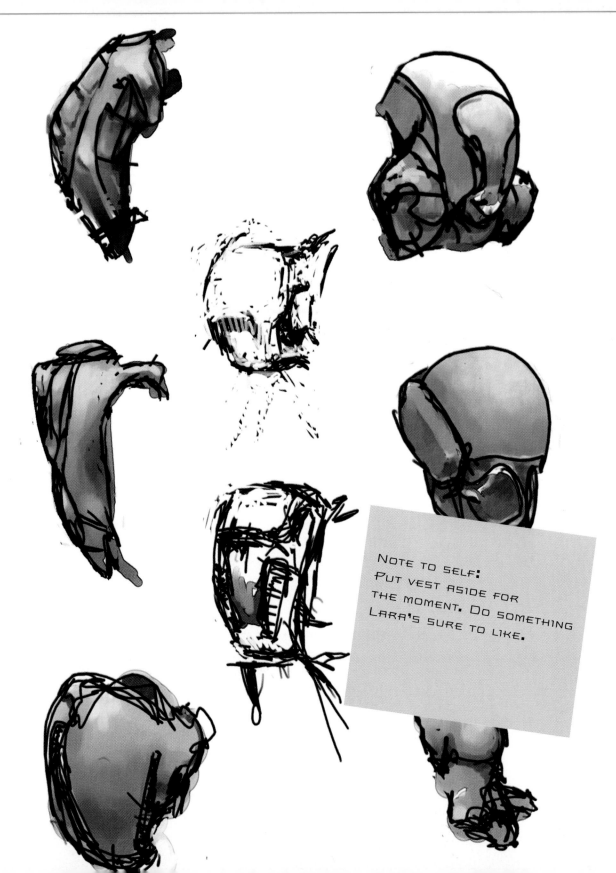

NOTE TO SELF:
PUT VEST ASIDE FOR
THE MOMENT. DO SOMETHING
LARA'S SURE TO LIKE.

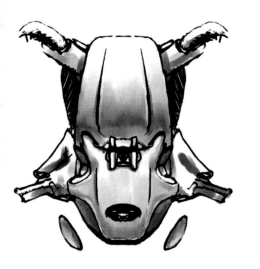

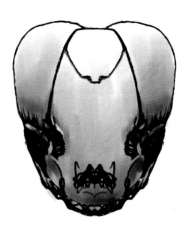

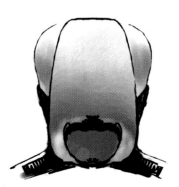

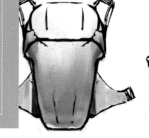

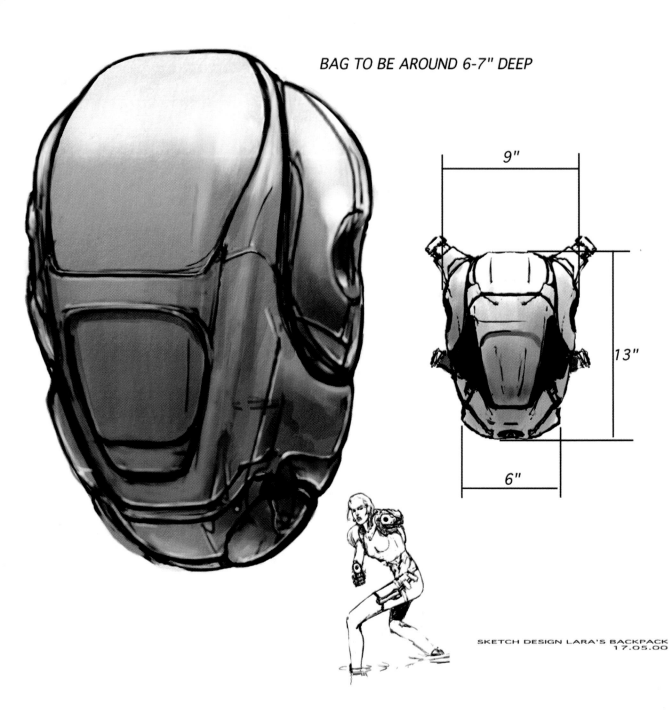

BAG TO BE AROUND 6-7" DEEP

9"

13"

6"

SKETCH DESIGN LARA'S BACKPACK
17.05.00

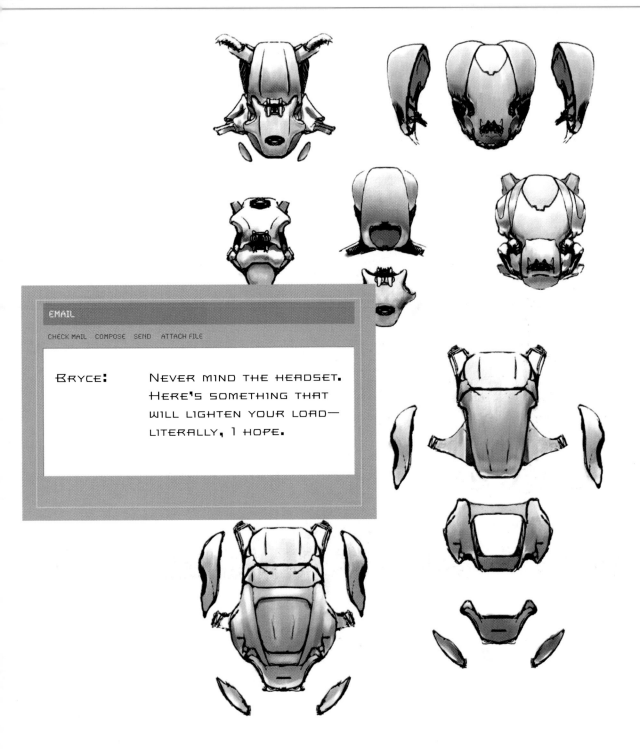

SKETCH DESIGN LARA'S BACKPACK
17.05.00

BRYCE: I KNOW, I KNOW YOU ALREADY HAVE A BACKPACK,
BUT IT'S OLDER THAN YOU ARE.
THE ONLY THING IT'S STILL GOOD FOR IS TARGET PRACTICE.

LIVE FEED

00:00:00

POWER   RECORD PLAY REWIND FORWARD

BRYCE: EXHIBIT A, A STAINLESS-STEEL KNIFE—
         NOT THAT YOU WOULD EVER HANG ONTO IT
         LONG ENOUGH TO WORRY ABOUT RUST.

LIVE FEED

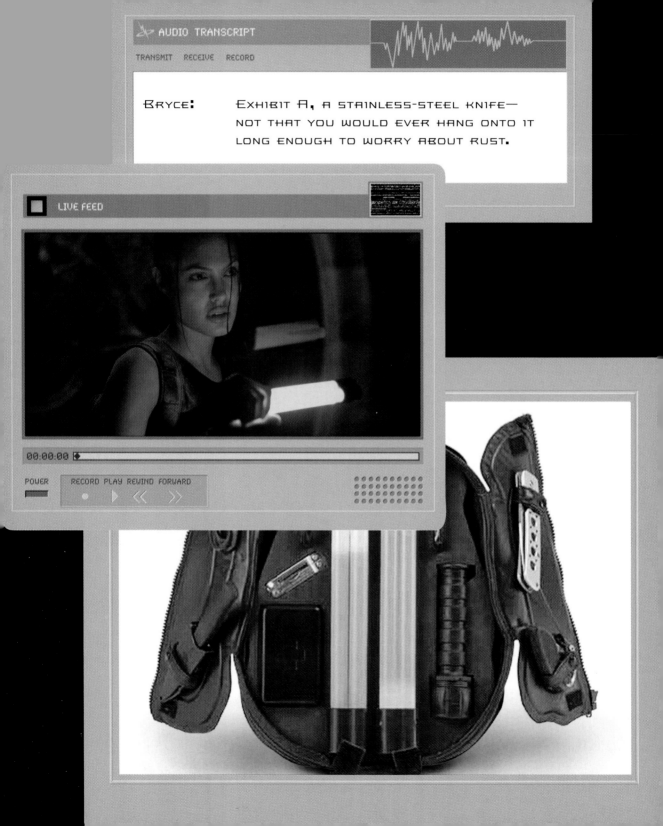

00:00:00 ▶

POWER   RECORD PLAY REWIND FORWARD
          ●   ▶   ≪   ≫

⚑ AUDIO TRANSCRIPT

TRANSMIT   RECEIVE   RECORD

BRYCE: EXHIBIT B, CHEMICAL FLARES. GOOD FOR THOSE
         AWKWARD TIMES WHEN YOU'RE DOWN TO EATING
         COCKROACHES AND YOU WOULDN'T MIND BEING
         SPOTTED BY A PASSING HELICOPTER.

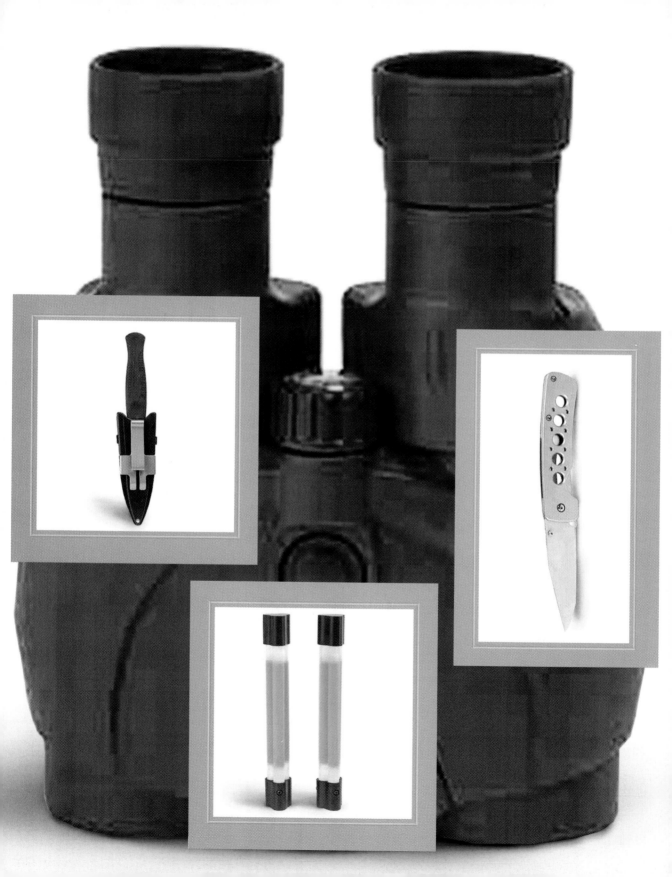

AUDIO TRANSCRIPT

TRANSMIT   RECEIVE   RECORD

BRYCE: EXHIBIT C, HIGH-POWERED BINOCULARS WITH INFRARED LENSES.
          WITH THESE BLIGHTERS, YOU COULD MAKE OUT A FRUIT FLY AT
          A HUNDRED METERS.

BRYCE: EXHIBIT D, HIGH-TENSILE CLIMBING ROPES, GUARANTEED TO CARRY
          FIVE HUNDRED KILOS OR YOUR MONEY BACK.

00:00:00

POWER   RECORD PLAY REWIND FORWARD

BRYCE: AND IT ALL PACKS UP INSIDE THIS SMART-LOOKING,
            SHOCK-ABSORBENT, INJECTION-MOLDED BACKPACK,
            ONE SIZE FITS ALL.

EMAIL   FILE ATTACHED

CHECK MAIL   COMPOSE   SEND   ATTACH FILE

LARA: YOU'VE FORGOTTEN JUST ONE THING.
            I MAY NEED EXTRA AMMUNITION.

EMAIL

CHECK MAIL   COMPOSE   SEND.   ATTACH FILE

BRYCE: ALL RIGHT, THEN. WHAT ABOUT A BANDOLIER TREE?
           IT CAN EXTEND FROM THE BOTTOM OF THE PACK.
           IT WOULDN'T WEIGH TOO MUCH—NOT MUCH MORE
           THAN YOUR .45s. AND WHILE WE'RE ON THE SUBJECT
           OF GUN HOLSTERS . . .

INSTANT MESSAGE

FILE   EDIT   INSERT   PEOPLE

LARA: I DON'T NEED NEW HOLSTERS.

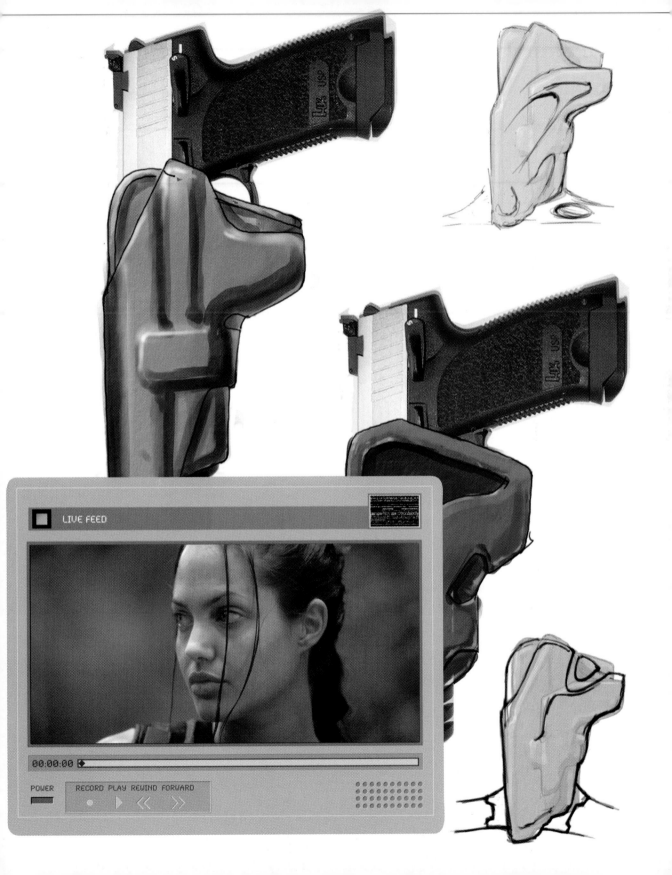

LIVE FEED

00:00:00

POWER   RECORD PLAY REWIND FORWARD

BRYCE: HOW ABOUT A HARNESS THAT
           WILL KEEP YOUR GUNS AT YOUR
           SIDE EVEN IF YOUR BELT GETS
           RIPPED TO SHREDS? I WORKED
           SO HARD ON IT.

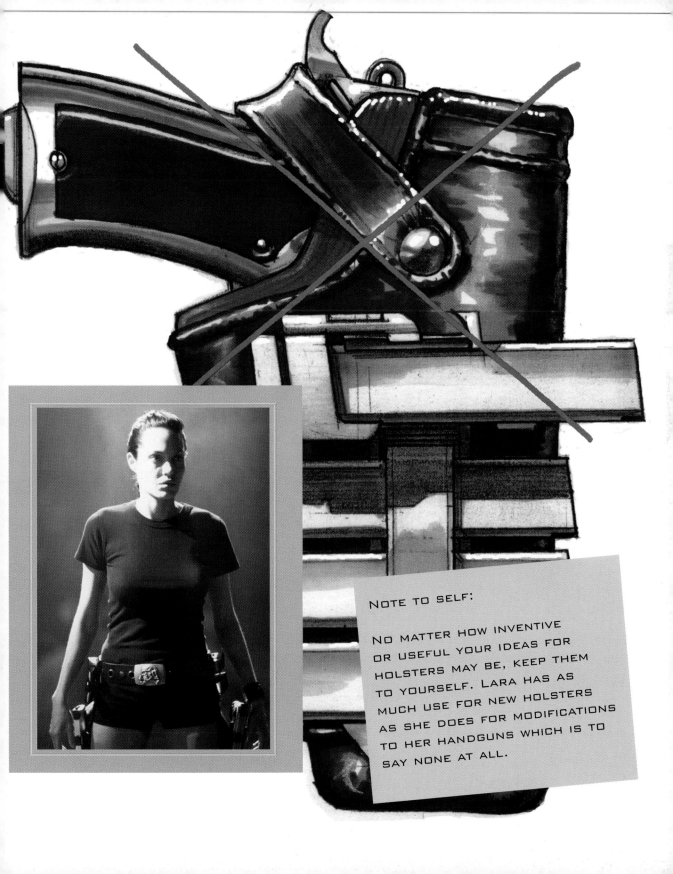

NOTE TO SELF:

NO MATTER HOW INVENTIVE OR USEFUL YOUR IDEAS FOR HOLSTERS MAY BE, KEEP THEM TO YOURSELF. LARA HAS AS MUCH USE FOR NEW HOLSTERS AS SHE DOES FOR MODIFICATIONS TO HER HANDGUNS WHICH IS TO SAY NONE AT ALL.

FILE   EDIT   INSERT   PEOPLE

BRYCE: GUESS WHAT?
         I'VE MADE UP SOME NEW HEADSET DESIGNS.

LARA: I WAS WONDERING WHEN YOU WOULD GET AROUND TO THAT.

BRYCE: CARE TO SEE THEM?

LARA: TEN MINUTES, IN THE LIBRARY.

INSTANT MESSAGE

FILE EDIT INSERT PEOPLE

LARA: RIGHT NOW, I'M STUDYING MARS.

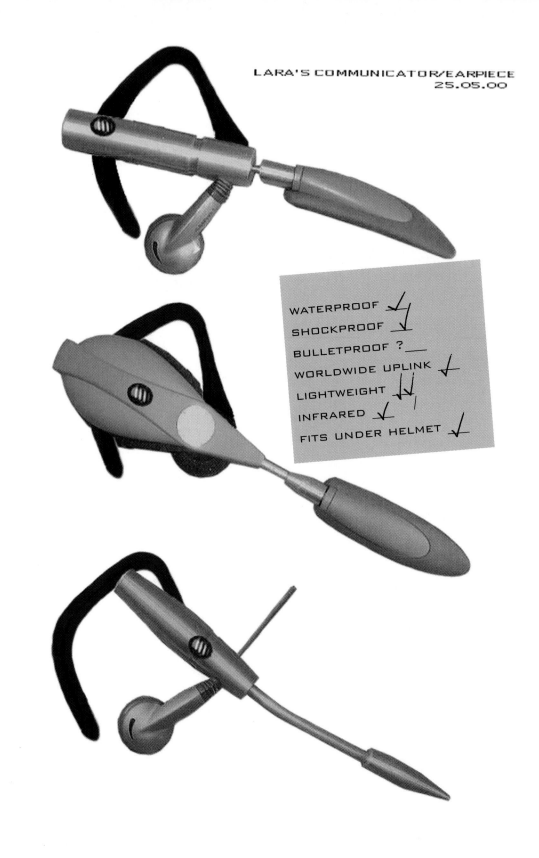

WATERPROOF ✓
SHOCKPROOF ✓
BULLETPROOF ?___
WORLDWIDE UPLINK ✓
LIGHTWEIGHT ✓
INFRARED ✓
FITS UNDER HELMET ✓

BRYCE: You like that one? 1 should have known.

LARA: Why do you say that?

BRYCE: It's the least attractive of the lot.

LARA CROFT'S COMMUNICATOR/ EARPIECE
26.05.00

FILE   EDIT   INSERT   PEOPLE

BRYCE: Not that it's any of my business, but what were you
          doing in the dumbwaiter?

LARA: Seeing if it still works. One never knows when such
          a thing will come in handy.

BRYCE: But it's so low-tech.

LARA: And that's bad?

BRYCE: Which reminds me—it's high time you had some new wheels.

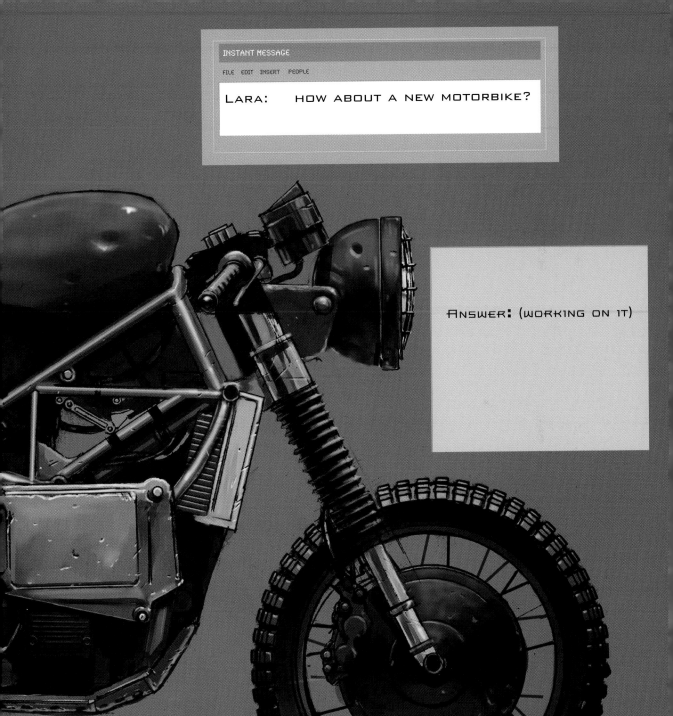

INSTANT MESSAGE

FILE   EDIT   INSERT   PEOPLE

LARA: HOW ABOUT A NEW MOTORBIKE?

ANSWER: (WORKING ON IT)

NOTE TO SELF:

LAY OFF JUNK FOOD
AFTER 2 A.M.

LARA: KIPPING OFF? IS THIS WHAT I'M PAYING YOU FOR?

BRYCE: THINKING, LARA, I WAS THINKING.

LARA: ABOUT WHAT? THE INSIDE OF YOUR EYELIDS?

EMAIL

CHECK MAIL   COMPOSE   SEND.   ATTACH FILE

BRYCE: LADY CROFT IS KINDLY INVITED
            TO VISIT THE ROAD BEHIND THE
            MANOR, WHERE SHE WILL NO DOUBT
            BE PLEASED AND AMAZED BY HER
            UNDERLING'S HANDIWORK.

AUDIO TRANSCRIPT

TRANSMIT RECEIVE RECORD

BRYCE: BEAUTIFUL, ISN'T SHE? A WORK OF
           ART, IF I SAY SO MYSELF.

LARA: SPEED?

LIVE FEED

00:00:00

POWER

RECORD PLAY REWIND FORWARD

AUDIO TRANSCRIPT

TRANSMIT RECEIVE RECORD

LARA: WILL SHE HANDLE
          THE BUMPS?

BRYCE: SHE'LL HANDLE THE
          DARK SIDE OF THE
          MOON, IF YOU LIKE.

LARA: I DON'T THINK I'LL
          BE GOING THAT FAR,
          THOUGH OF COURSE,
          ONE NEVER KNOWS.

LIVE FEED

00:00:00

POWER   RECORD PLAY REWIND FORWARD

AUDIO TRANSCRIPT

TRANSMIT RECEIVE RECORD

BRYCE: IN CASE YOU WERE WONDERING,
          THE STRAPS ARE FOR YOUR
          BACKPACK.

LARA: AND THE NETTING?

BRYCE: FOR WHATEVER ELSE YOU
          MAY CARE TO CARRY WITH YOU.

AUDIO TRANSCRIPT

TRANSMIT   RECEIVE   RECORD

BRYCE: AND, 1 ASK YOU—WHAT WOULD
A BIKE BE WITHOUT SOME
FIRST-CLASS LEATHERS?

LARA: YOU'RE TOO GOOD TO ME, BRYCIE.

BRYCE: HAVEN'T 1 BEEN TELLING YOU THAT ALL ALONG?

AUDIO TRANSCRIPT

TRANSMIT   RECEIVE   RECORD

BRYCE: NOTE THE PADDED BITS.
              THAT'S WHERE YOU WORE OUT THE LAST OUTFIT,
              MAY IT <u>REST</u> IN PEACE.

AUDIO TRANSCRIPT

TRANSMIT   RECEIVE   RECORD

BRYCE: THE HELMET'S THE BEST PART.

LARA: IS THAT A COMM UNIT?

BRYCE: THE BEST GPS TECHNOLOGY THE PENTAGON'S MONEY CAN BUY.

LARA: YOU STOLE THIS FROM THE PENTAGON?

BRYCE: ACTUALLY, 1 JUST BORROWED IT.

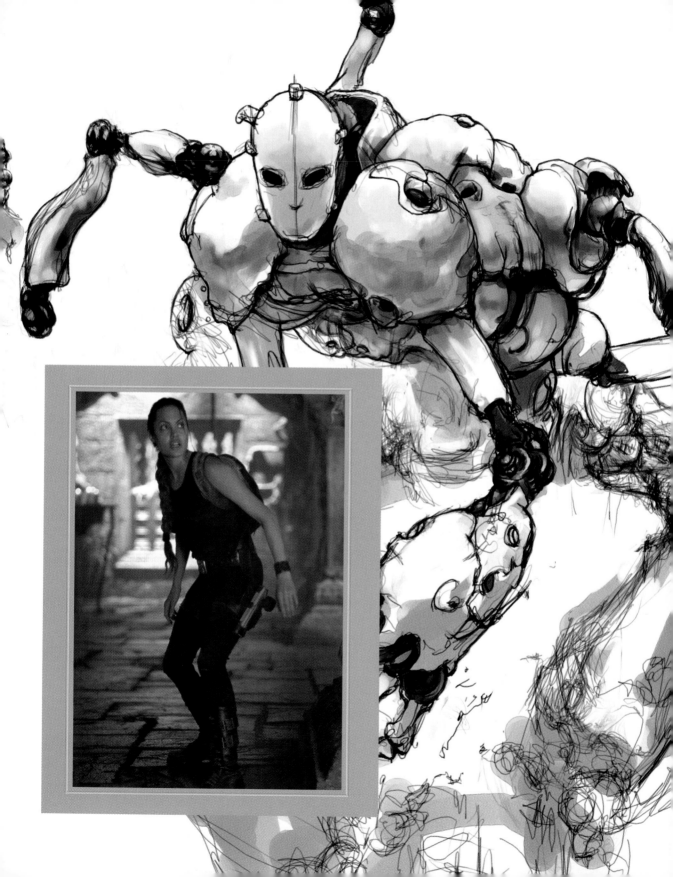

H

NOTE TO SELF:

LARA LIKES THE MOTORCYCLE
ENSEMBLE. NOW WOULD
BE A GOOD TIME TO ASK
FOR A RAISE ALSO, TO
REVISIT THE ROBOT IDEA.

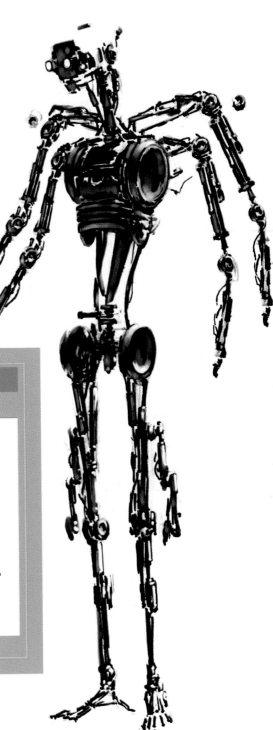

INSTANT MESSAGE

FILE EDIT INSERT. PEOPLE

BRYCE: SAY SOMETHING.

LARA: IT'S GOT TOO MANY
ARMS. THEY'LL JUST
GET IN THE WAY.

BRYCE: BUT YOU WANTED
APPENDAGES THAT
COULD CUT AND FIRE.

LARA: NOT ALL AT ONCE.

00:00:00

POWER   RECORD PLAY REWIND FORWARD

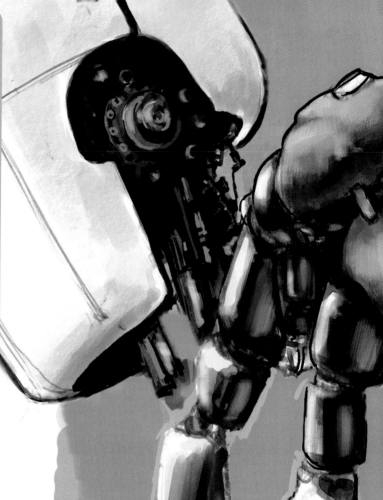

INSTANT MESSAGE

FILE   EDIT   INSERT   PEOPLE

BRYCE: HOW ABOUT NOW?

LARA: THAT MASK LOOKS LIKE SOMETHING
            AN AMERICAN HOCKEY GOALIE MIGHT WEAR.

BRYCE: GET RID OF IT?

LARA: YOU READ MY MIND.

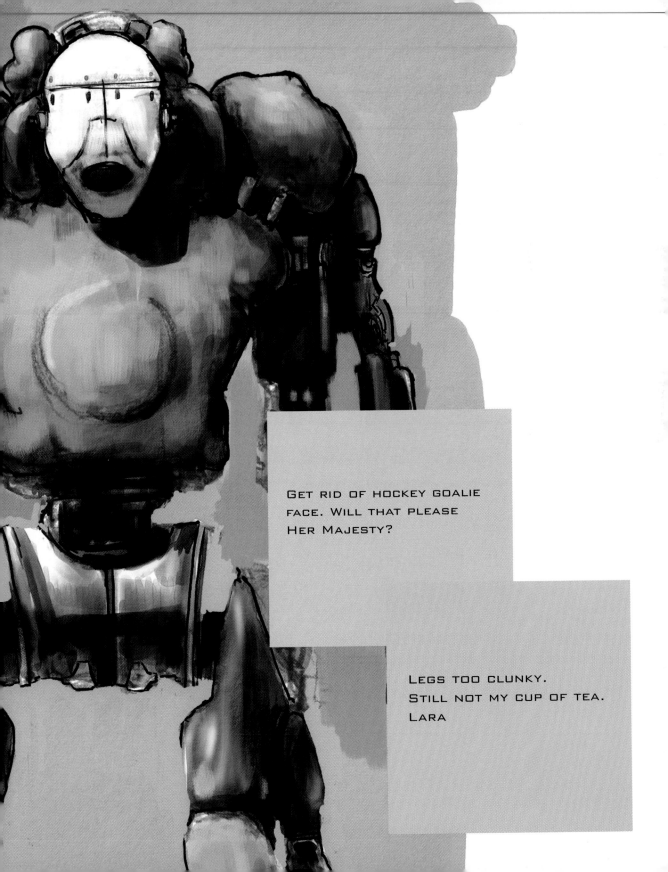

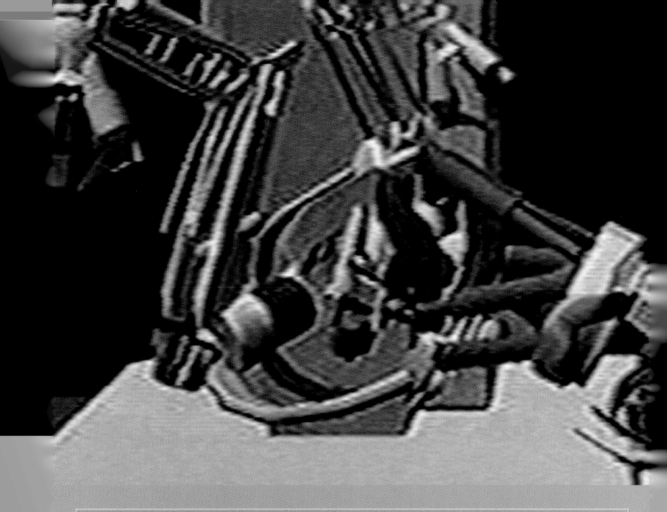

INSTANT MESSAGE

FILE EDIT INSERT PEOPLE

BRYCE: LARA, MY GREAT AUNT PETUNIA WAS SPINDLY. THIS ROBOT IS SLEEK AND STREAMLINED.

LARA: AND SPINDLY. I COULD SEVER ITS HEAD FROM ITS NECK WITH A HALF-DOZEN SLUGS.

BRYCE: MUM WAS RIGHT. I SHOULD HAVE GOTTEN A <u>REAL JOB</u>.

LIVE FEED

00:00:00

POWER   RECORD PLAY REWIND FORWARD

BRYCE: HERE. I TOOK THE LIBERTY OF PROVIDING YOU
        WITH NEW SUNGLASSES. POLARIZED, OF COURSE.
        AND EXTRA IMPACT-RESISTANT.

LARA: YOU MADE A PAIR OF GLASSES FOR ME?
        I DIDN'T KNOW YOUR TALENTS EXTENDED
        TO GRINDING LENSES.

BRYCE: THEY DON'T. I BOUGHT THE SILLY THINGS
        AT HARROD'S.

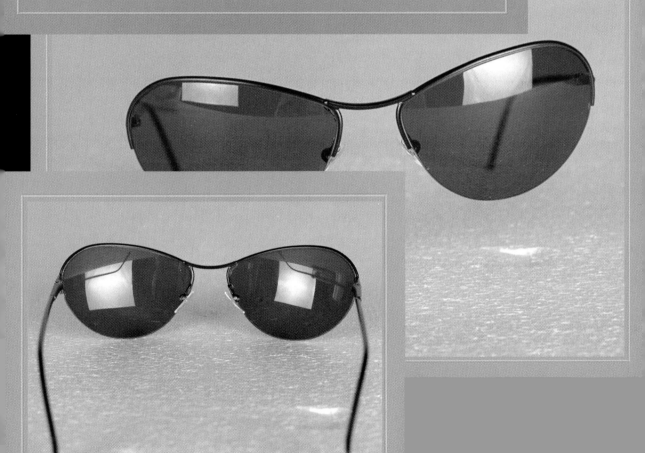

INSTANT MESSAGE

FILE EDIT INSERT PEOPLE

LARA: A GAS MASK?

BRYCE: YOU NEVER KNOW WHEN
          YOU MIGHT NEED ONE.

LARA: I'VE GOTTEN BY WITHOUT IT.

BRYCE: MAYBE YOU'VE BEEN LUCKY.

FILE EDIT INSERT. PEOPLE

LARA: IT'S TOO CLUMSY. WHERE WOULD I PUT IT?

BRYCE: FOR ALL I CARE, YOU CAN SH—

LARA: DON'T BE SNIPPY, LOVE.

BRYCE: I KNOW. PERHAPS HILLARY WOULD LIKE ONE.

LARA: THERE'S THE SPIRIT.

NOTE TO SELF:

IT'S BEEN A WHILE
SINCE LARA HAD A
NEW PARACHUTE.

INSTANT MESSAGE

FILE   EDIT   INSERT   PEOPLE

BRYCE: MAY I SEE YOU IN THE LAB?

LARA: IN A MOMENT.

BRYCE: DON'T TELL ME, YOU'RE IN THE TELESCOPE AGAIN.

LARA: GOOD GUESS.

BRYCE: STUDYING MARS?

LARA: BETELGEUSE, ACTUALLY—AS IF IT WERE
            ANY OF YOUR BUSINESS.

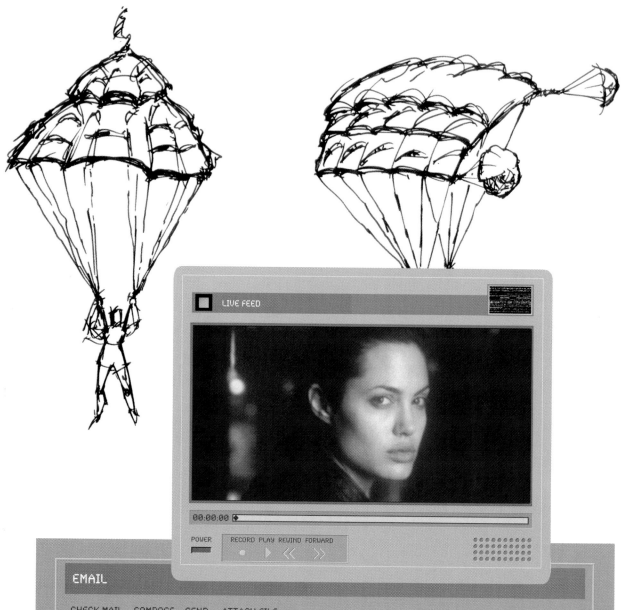

LIVE FEED

00:00:00

POWER   RECORD PLAY REWIND FORWARD

EMAIL

CHECK MAIL   COMPOSE   SEND.   ATTACH FILE

BRYCE: EVEN YOU CAN APPRECIATE THE OCCASIONAL
            SOFT LANDING, MY DEAR. COMMENT? CRITICISM?

LARA: YOU'VE GOT WAY TOO MUCH TIME ON YOUR HANDS,
            BRYCIE. I'LL STICK WITH ROYAL AIR FORCE SURPLUS.

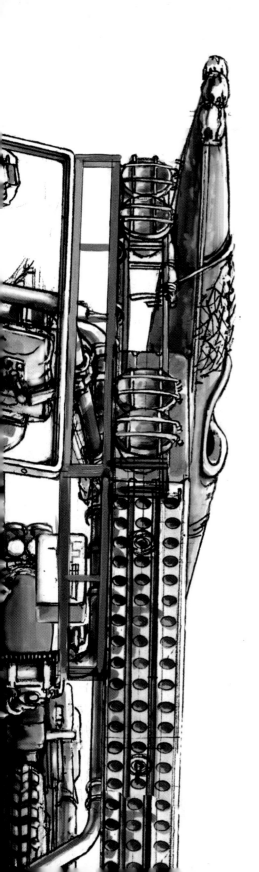

Add a kayak,
just in case the monsoons get out of
control. And a heavier front bumper
will protect it from some of the
punishment it's bound to take.

AUDIO TRANSCRIPT

TRANSMIT   RECEIVE   RECORD

BRYCE: JOIN ME IN THE GARAGE, WILL YOU?
            YOUR CHARIOT AWAITS.

LARA: I'M FINISHING UP IN THE DARKROOM.
            BE THERE PRESENTLY.

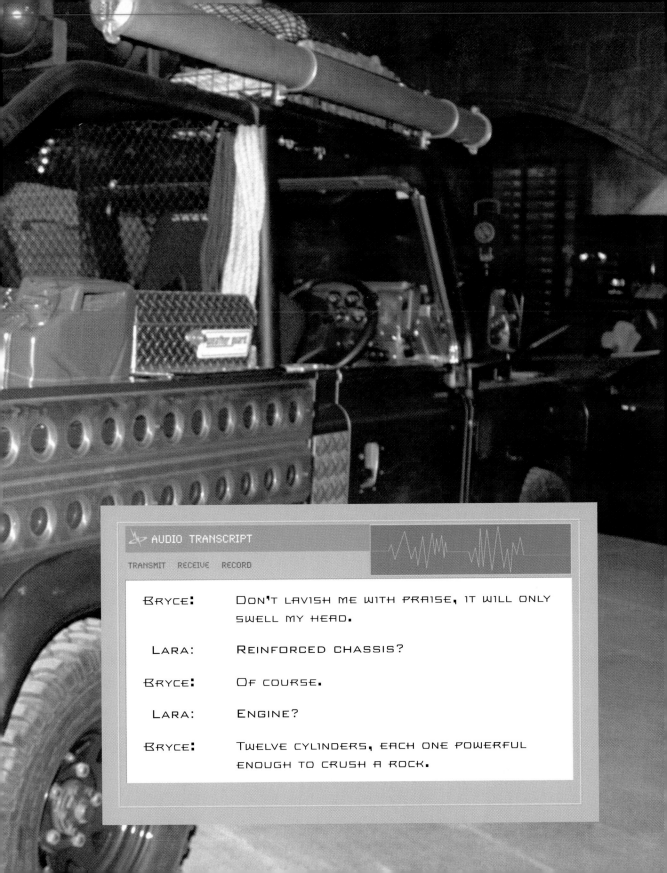

AUDIO TRANSCRIPT

TRANSMIT   RECEIVE   RECORD

BRYCE: DON'T LAVISH ME WITH PRAISE, IT WILL ONLY SWELL MY HEAD.

LARA: REINFORCED CHASSIS?

BRYCE: OF COURSE.

LARA: ENGINE?

BRYCE: TWELVE CYLINDERS, EACH ONE POWERFUL ENOUGH TO CRUSH A ROCK.

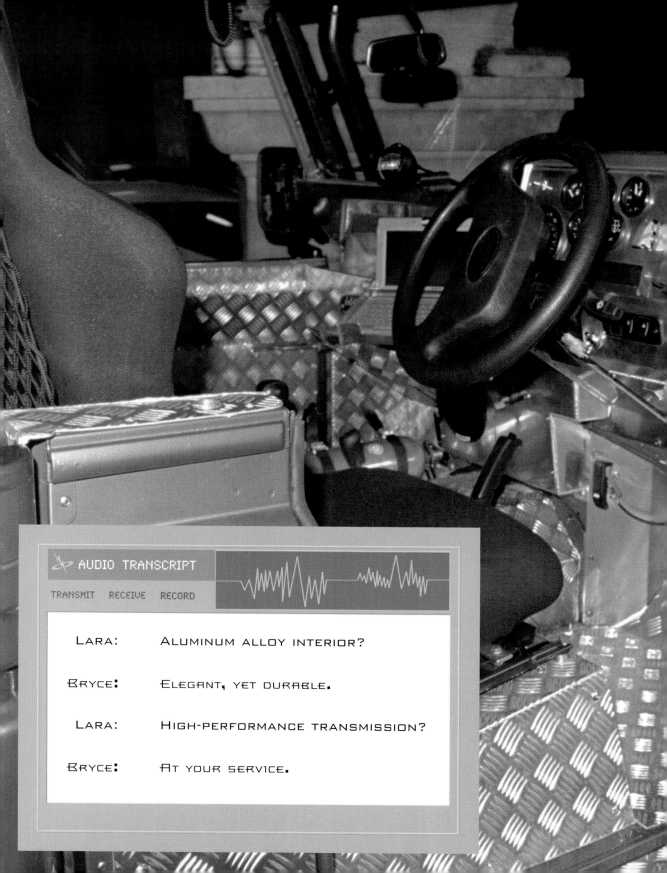

AUDIO TRANSCRIPT

TRANSMIT   RECEIVE   RECORD

LARA: ALUMINUM ALLOY INTERIOR?

BRYCE: ELEGANT, YET DURABLE.

LARA: HIGH-PERFORMANCE TRANSMISSION?

BRYCE: AT YOUR SERVICE.

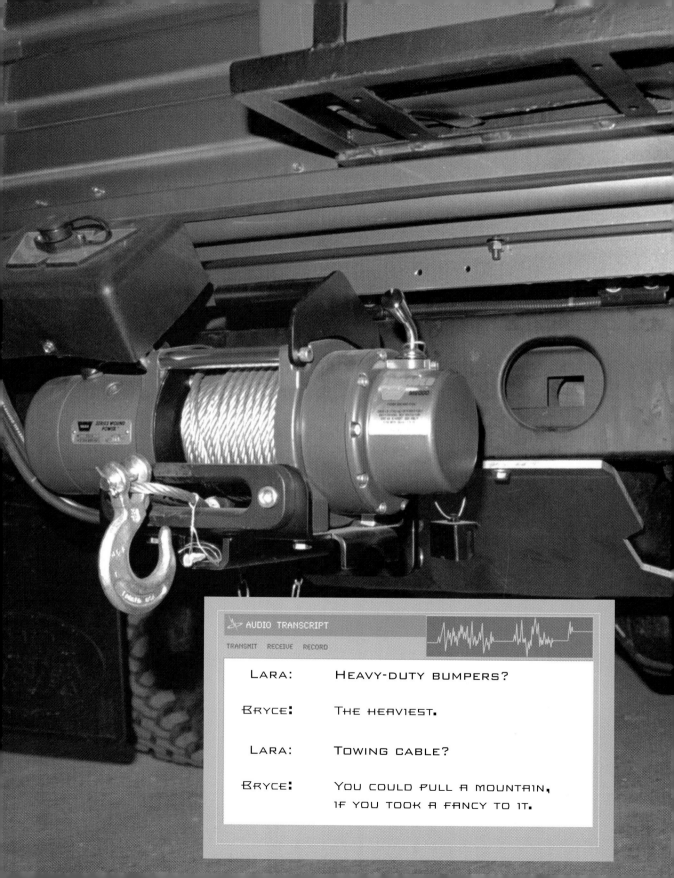

LIVE FEED

00:00:00

POWER   RECORD PLAY REWIND FORWARD

AUDIO TRANSCRIPT

TRANSMIT   RECEIVE   RECORD

LARA: YOU'VE OUTDONE YOURSELF, BRYCIE.

BRYCE: THEN YOU LIKE IT?

LARA: LET ME SLEEP ON IT.

00:0(

POWER

NOTE TO SELF:

WHILE LARA'S BASKING
IN THE GLOW OF HER NEW
LAND ROVER, MODIFY ROBOT
TO SUIT HER WHIMS. THE THINGS
I DO FOR THAT WOMAN . . .

EMAIL   FILE ATTACHED

CHECK MAIL   COMPOSE   SEND   ATTACH FILE

BRYCE: YOUR ROBOT AWAITS.

LARA: YOU'VE GOT SKETCHES?

BRYCE: I'VE GOT BETTER THAN SKETCHES.

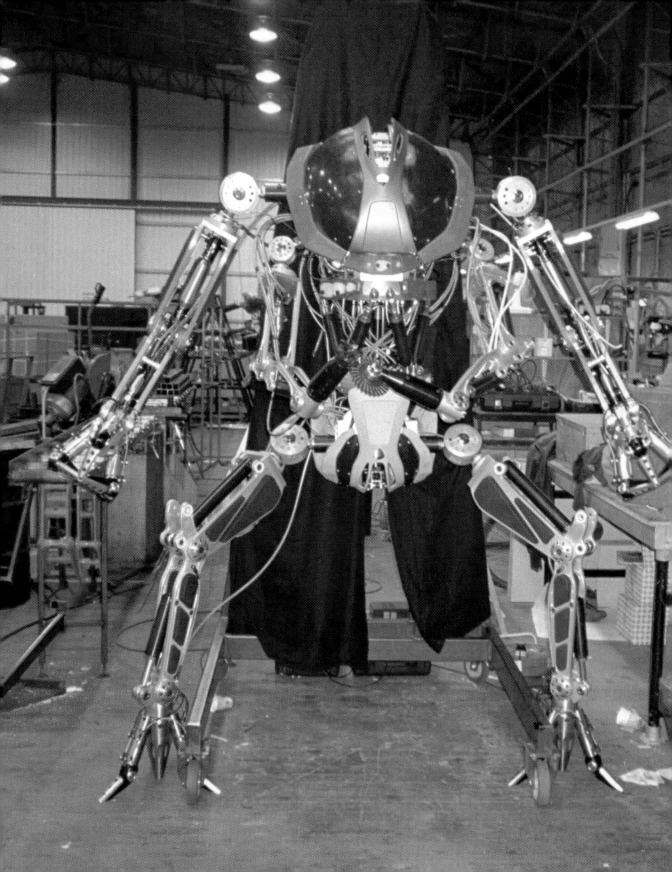

FILE ATTACHED

CHECK MAIL   COMPOSE   SEND.   ATTACH FILE

BRYCE: TELL ME YOU DON'T LOVE THIS. 1 DARE YOU.

LARA: I DO LOVE IT.

BRYCE: YOU DO? 1 MEAN, ER, OF COURSE YOU DO.

LARA: ON THE OUTSIDE, THAT IS.

BRYCE: BUT AN OUTSIDE IS ALL IT HAS AT THE MOMENT.

LARA: THEN YOU HAD BEST GET AROUND TO WORKING
         ON ITS INSIDES, HADN'T YOU?

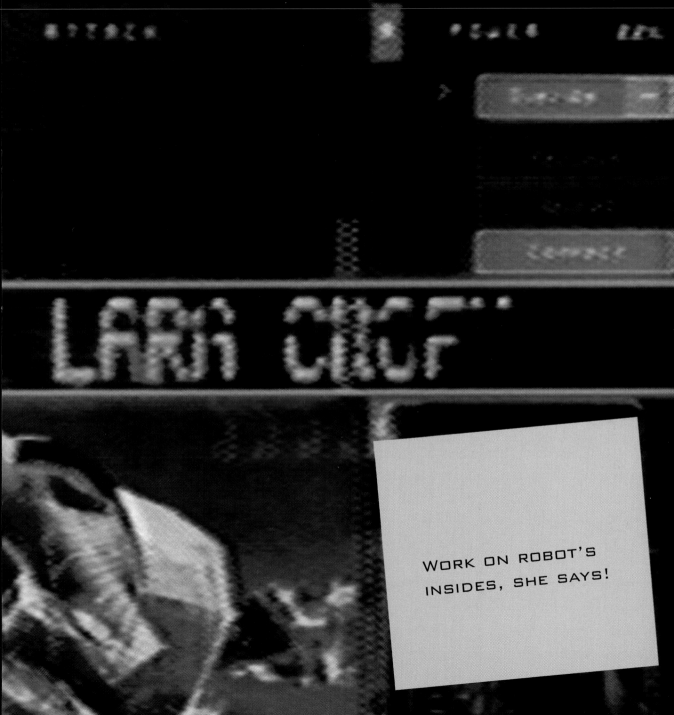

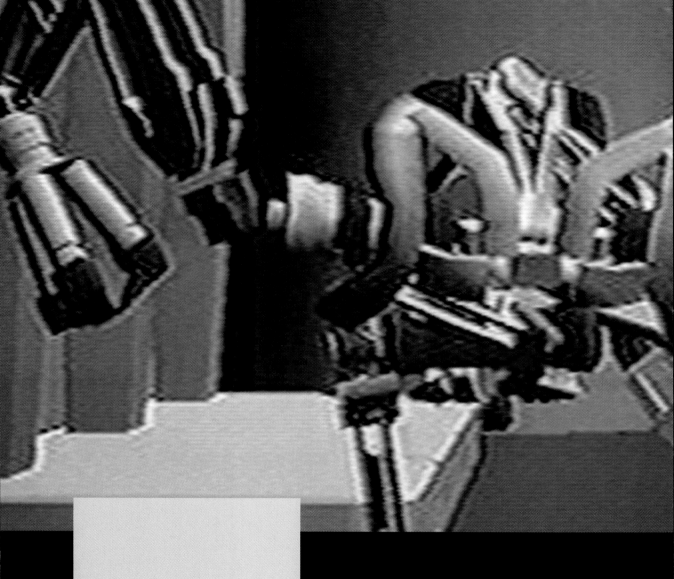

1) FINE-TUNE STEALTH MODE.

2) STABILIZE OPTICS.

3) CALL FOR PIZZA.

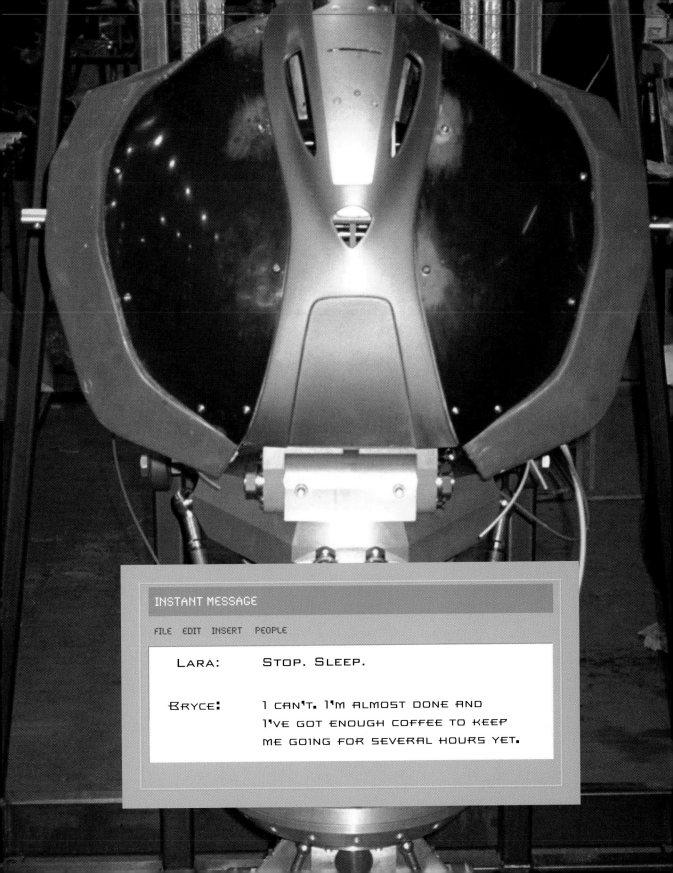

INSTANT MESSAGE

FILE EDIT INSERT PEOPLE

LARA: STOP. SLEEP.

BRYCE: I CAN'T. I'M ALMOST DONE AND
          I'VE GOT ENOUGH COFFEE TO KEEP
          ME GOING FOR SEVERAL HOURS YET.

POWER

joules

MIN   MAX

hammer

12%   DAMAGE ASSESSMENT

drill

error   CONSIDER
                                Robot

fire

88%

knives

34%

Weapons

chuck

error   SIMULATION ABORTED, L

Weapons

RESULTS

Video   thermal

                error   VIEW

                night

                15%   FRONT

Video   gamma

                51%

                M.R.I

                spine

PROGRAM   STEALTH   HOLD   RETREAT   ANALYS

LARA: IT'S GOT INSIDES?

BRYCE: BLOODY RIGHT IT'S GOT INSIDES. CARE TO TAKE IT FOR A SPIN?

LARA: SOON ENOUGH.

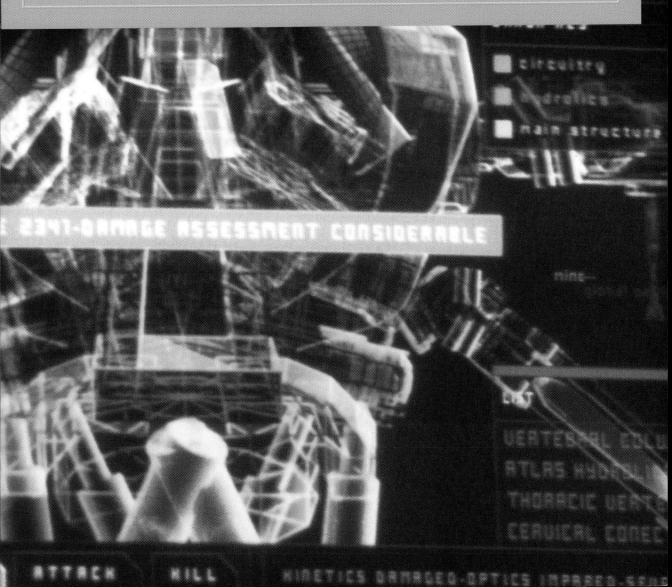

  FILE ATTACHED

CHECK MAIL   COMPOSE   SEND   ATTACH FILE

BRYCE: YOU KNOW HOW YOU'RE ALWAYS COMPLAINING THAT YOU
         DON'T GET ENOUGH EXERCISE AROUND HERE?

LARA: YOU'RE BUILDING ME A GYM?

BRYCE: EVEN BETTER.

LARA: BUNGEE CORDS? IN THE GRAND HALL?

BRYCE: NOT WHAT THE ORIGINAL ARCHITECT INTENDED,
            I'LL GRANT YOU. BUT SMASHING NONETHELESS.

CHECK MAIL   COMPOSE   SEND.   ATTACH FILE

BRYCE: Imagine yourself flying through the air,
         immersing yourself in the haunting melody of
         a Bach concerto.

LARA: I'll admit the idea appeals to me. I can just see the
         look on the face of the UPS man.

EMAIL

CHECK MAIL   COMPOSE   SEND   ATTACH FILE

BRYCE: TRY THEM OUT.

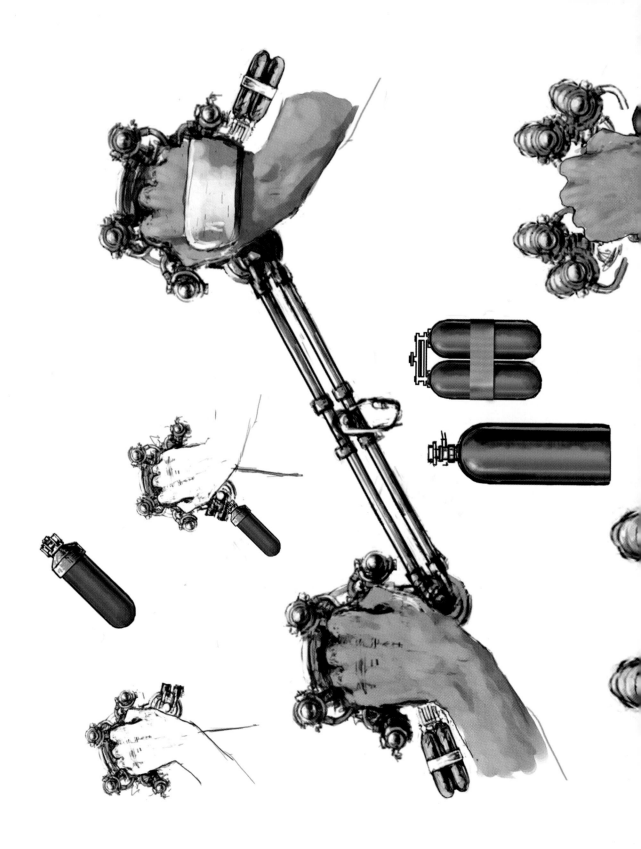

CHECK MAIL   COMPOSE   SEND   ATTACH FILE

LARA:	CLIMBING GEAR, EH?
BRYCE:	FOR SCALING THOSE HARD-TO-SCALE SURFACES.
LARA:	I CAN BE THE FLY ON THE WALL, THEN?
BRYCE:	ON THE WALL, ON THE CEILING, ON THE CHANDELIER—IF YOU LIKE.

AUDIO TRANSCRIPT

TRANSMIT   RECEIVE   RECORD

LARA: THANKS, BRYCE. I FEEL PREPARED TO TAKE ON
         THE WORLD AGAIN.

BRYCE: JUST THE WORLD? I'LL HAVE TO WORK A LITTLE HARDER.

LARA: YOU DO THAT.

AUDIO TRANSCRIPT

TRANSMIT   RECEIVE   RECORD

LARA: AND I'LL MAKE SURE
           NEITHER OF US EVER
           GETS BORED.